# RACHEL ISADORA

VIKING

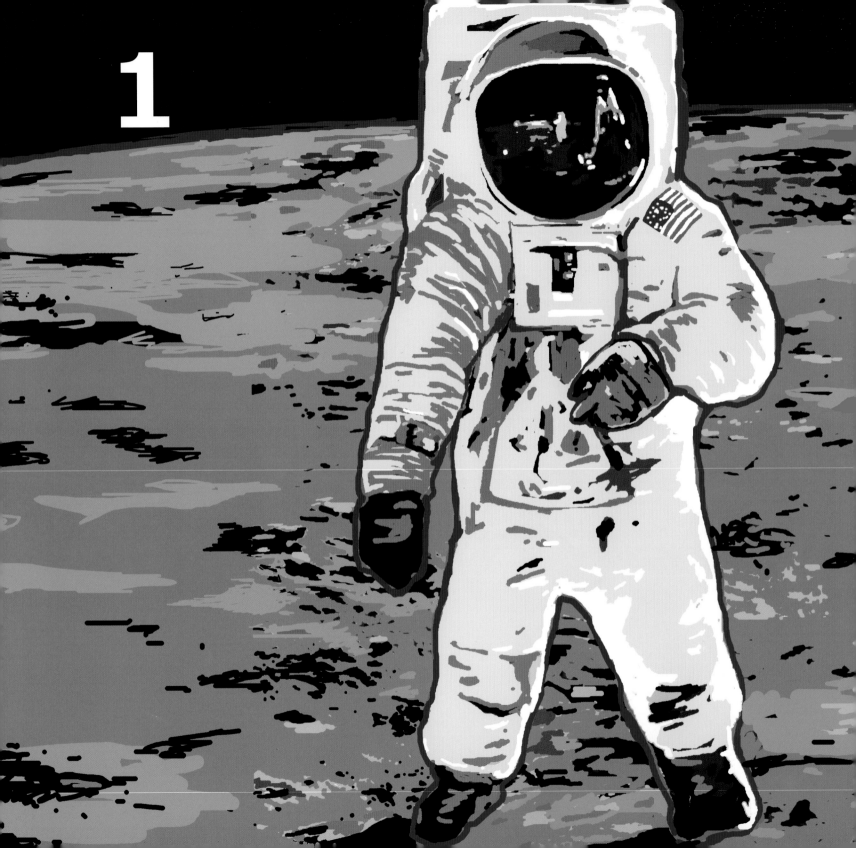

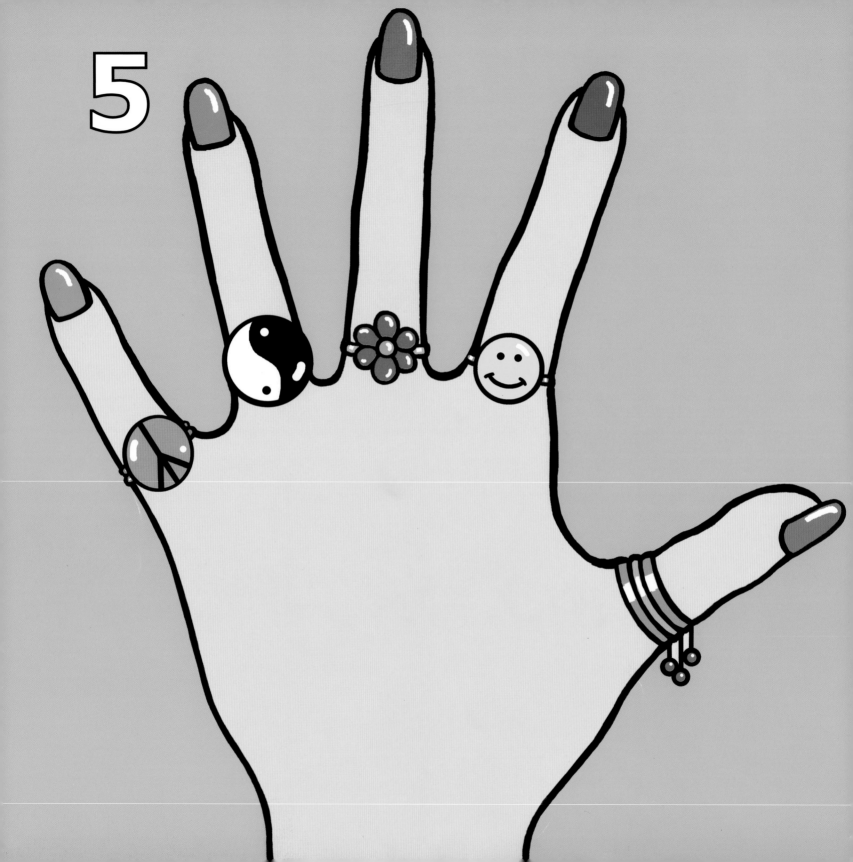

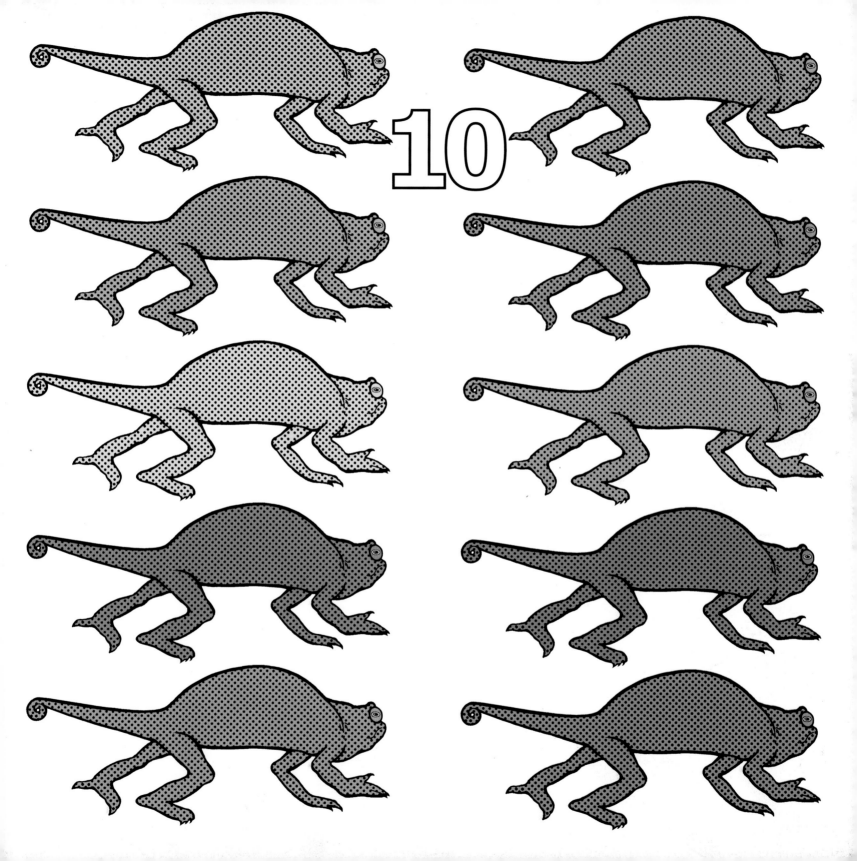

10

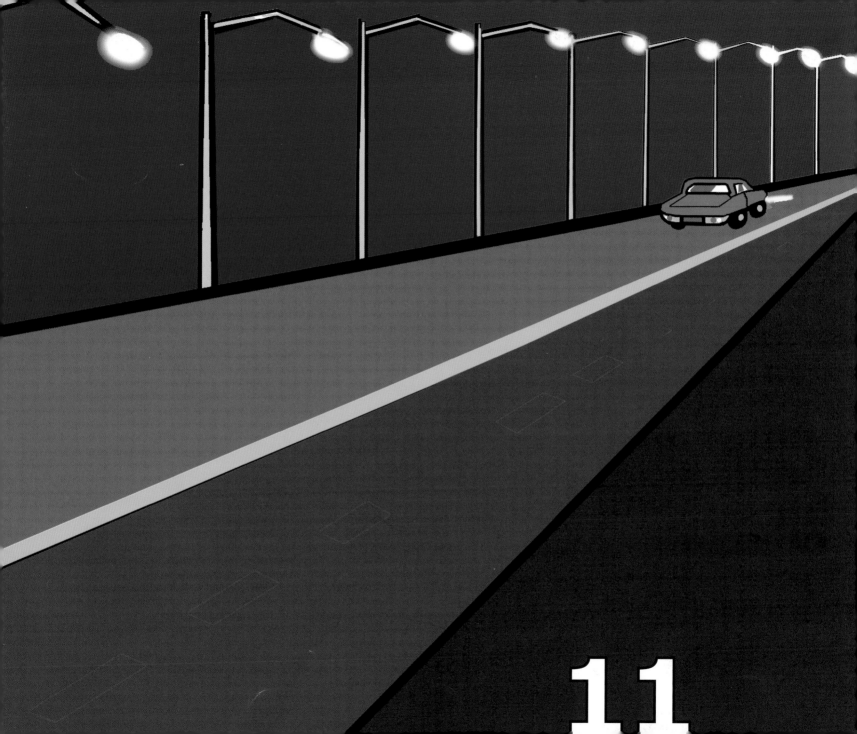

11

12

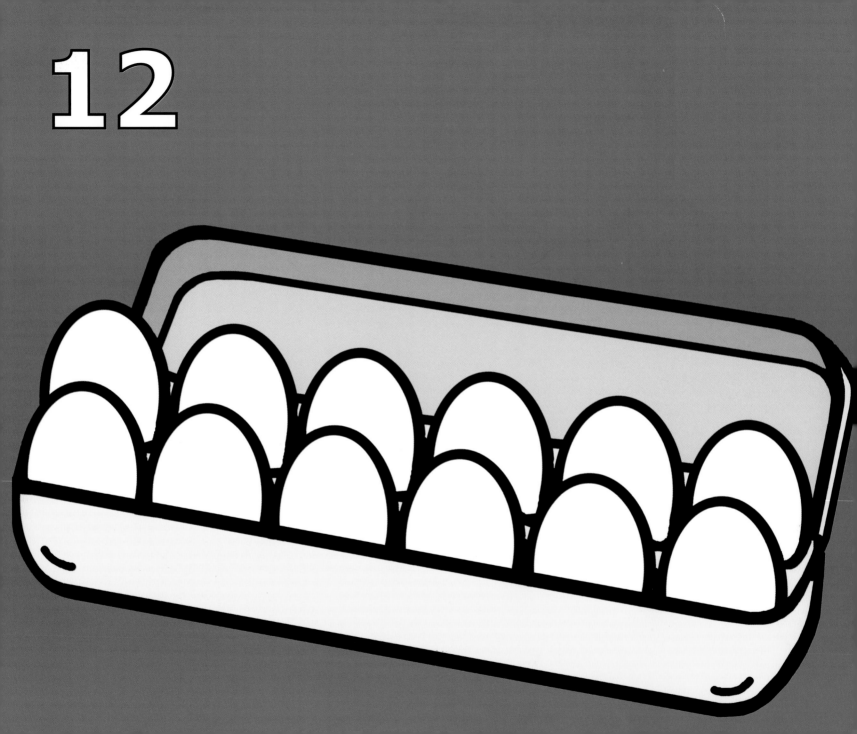

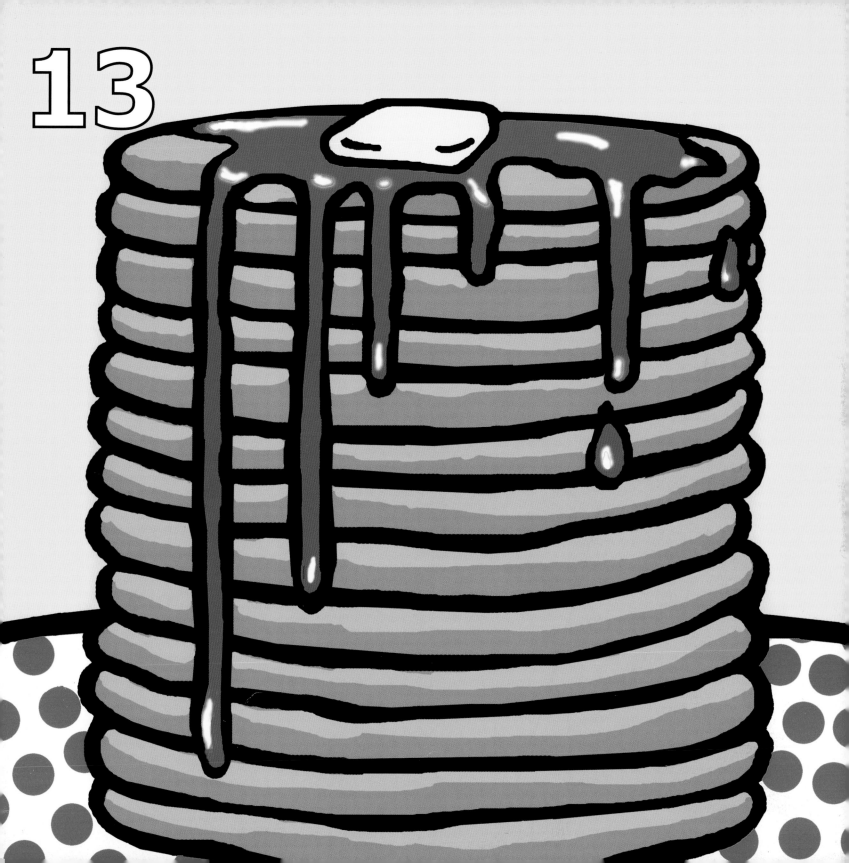

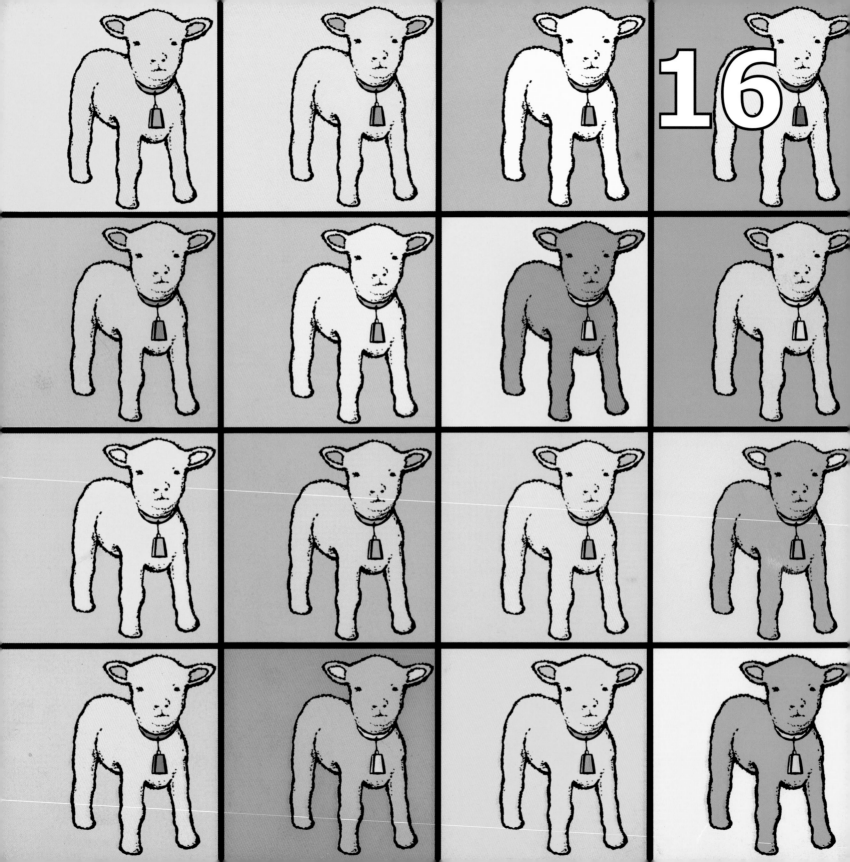

20

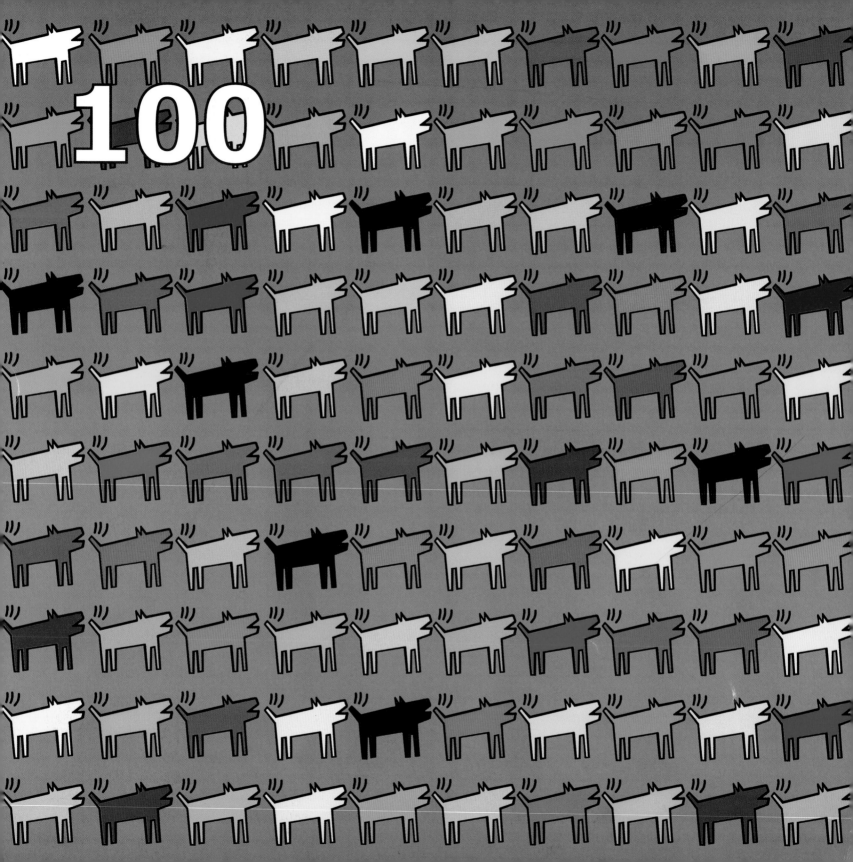

100

1,000

VIKING
Published by the Penguin Group
Penguin Putnam Books for Young Readers, 345 Hudson Street, New York, New York 10014, U.S.A.
Penguin Books Ltd, 27 Wrights Lane, London W8 5TZ, England
Penguin Books Australia Ltd, Ringwood, Victoria, Australia
Penguin Books Canada Ltd, 10 Alcorn Avenue, Toronto, Ontario, Canada M4V 3B2
Penguin Books (N.Z.) Ltd, 182-190 Wairau Road, Auckland 10, New Zealand

Penguin Books Ltd, Registered Offices: Harmondsworth, Middlesex, England

First published in 2000 by Viking, a member of Penguin Putnam Books for Young Readers.

1 3 5 7 9 10 8 6 4 2
Copyright © Rachel Isadora, 2000

LIBRARY OF CONGRESS CATALOGING-IN-PUBLICATION DATA
Isadora, Rachel.
123 pop! / by Rachel Isadora.
p.  cm.
Summary: Numbers from one to twenty and 500, 1000, and 10,000 are represented by illustrations in the pop art style.
ISBN 0-670-88859-1
1. Counting—Juvenile literature.  [1. Counting.] I. Title: 1 2 3 pop!. II. Title: One two three pop!.  III. Title.
QA113.I83  2000  513.2'11—dc21  99-056686

Printed in Hong Kong
Set in Tahoma